The Story of
OLD MRS. BRUBECK

and How
She Looked
for Trouble
and Where
She Found
Him

by LORE SEGAL · illustrated by MARCIA SEWALL

PANTHEON BOOKS

For Catherine and Elizabeth

Library of Congress Cataloging in Publication Data
Segal, Lore Groszmann. The story of Old Mrs. Brubeck and how she looked for trouble and where she found him.
Summary: Rather than have trouble catch her by surprise, a perpetual worrier deliberately looks for it.
[1. Worry—Fiction]   I. Sewall, Marcia.   II. Title.   PZ7.S4527St   [E]   78-31317   ISBN 0-394-84039-9   ISBN 0-394-94039-3 (lib. bdg.)

The Story of
OLD MRS. BRUBECK
and How She Looked for Trouble
and Where She Found Him

Old Mrs. Brubeck was a nervous person. She stacked her plates and hung her cups in rows the better to keep her eye out for trouble: Who can tell what might come leaping out or creeping from behind anything?

Old Mrs. Brubeck looked out the door. "Walk, Dearheart, don't run, you'll fall and hurt yourself," she called to her grandbaby, little Beatrix, a nice stout child with a brown braid down the middle of her back.

Then Mrs. Brubeck went to make her bed.

She spread the sheet and smoothed the
eiderdown because you never know what it
might be inside a fold or underneath a lump.
And it came to Mrs. Brubeck: What if the
ground humps suddenly underfoot and little
Beatrix trips and hurts herself? Old Mrs.
Brubeck ran to the window

and saw Beatrix perfectly all right, digging a hole with a stick.

Then it came to Mrs. Brubeck: Haven't I known trouble all my life? Don't I know the moment I look for a bump on the ground tripping up my darling, she might be rolling down a hole!

And Mrs. Brubeck ran to the door

but the grandbaby was perfectly fine, turning a somersault.

Old Mrs. Brubeck was walking back in the door when it came to her: What if trouble tricked me, keeping me looking for a bump or a hole in the ground, and all the time he's creeping up behind my darling to push her over?

Old Mrs. Brubeck quickly turned and ran out the door

and saw Beatrix sitting in the grass
eating a strawberry, and quite all right.

The old woman was turning to go in when
it came to her: Maybe that very moment,
while I looked for him in a bump or a hole
or creeping up behind my darling, trouble
was getting ready to drop on her head? "But
I know a trick or two!" said Mrs. Brubeck.
She made as if to go in the door, humming a
little song, and turned suddenly, and Beatrix
was perfectly fine, standing on her head.

"Just in the nick of time!" said the old woman. "You've got to get up pretty early in the morning to fool Grandmother Brubeck! I know what I'm going to do," said she. "I'm going to hide myself behind the door, and I'm going to keep my eye out for any trouble from a bump or a hole or creeping up behind or dropping down on Beatrix. Trouble won't have a moment in which he can come bothering my darling!"

By evening the poor woman was so tired she said, "There's got to be an end!
I am too old to wait for trouble another minute. I'm going after him!"
She took the grandbaby by the hand and said, "Come, Dearheart," and led
her in the door.

She gave her bread and milk for supper. Then she stacked the plate and hung the cup back on its hook, and when the grandbaby was safe asleep, Old Mrs. Brubeck set out to look for trouble.

"I'm going to find you too," she said, "after the life you've led me, if it's the last thing I do."

Old Mrs. Brubeck looked into the corner behind the stove, under the cupboard, and in every fold of every curtain. "Don't I know your ways?" she said. "The moment I come looking where you are, you're off to where I'm finished being."

"The truth is, I am worn out. I'm going to bed," said Mrs. Brubeck. And that is when she saw him, lying right there under her eiderdown! And she said, "Isn't that just like you to be where I'm not looking the moment I've forgotten all about you! Is this where you've been all this while, waiting for me?"

She gave him a long look and she said, "Nasty, aren't you! Why you are worse than I ever thought. But it's a blessed relief knowing what it is you are, after the chase you've led me all my life long. Now where d'you think you're going? Oh no you don't!" said Mrs. Brubeck, and she climbed into the bed and laid herself right down next to trouble.

She put her arm around him and she said, "So long as I've got you where I can keep my eye on you, I know you can't be troubling my darling, and I'm going to keep my eye on you as long as I live." She pulled up the blanket to cover the both of them.

But Mrs. Brubeck was tired; her eyes began to close. No sooner had her arm loosened from around his neck than trouble snuck out of that bed and left the house and didn't bother Mrs. Brubeck ever again.

Lore Segal

is the author of *Tell Me a Mitzi* and *Tell Me a Trudy,* and her translations include *The Juniper Tree,* a collection of stories from the Brothers Grimm, illustrated by Maurice Sendak. She was born in Vienna, educated at the University of London, and now commutes between her home in New York City and the University of Illinois in Chicago, where she teaches writing. She has two children, a son and a daughter.

Marcia Sewall

was born in Providence, Rhode Island, and graduated from Pembroke College of Brown University. She has taught art to high school students, worked at the Children's Museum in Boston, and is now a children's book illustrator. Her picture books include *The Nutcrackers and the Sugar-Tongs* by Edward Lear, *Come Again in the Spring, The Leprechaun's Story,* and *Crazy in Love,* all by Richard Kennedy. She lives in Boston, Massachusetts.